Fires

William B. Rice

Fires

Publishing Credits

Associate Editors
James Anderson
Torrey Maloof

Editorial Director
Dona Herweck Rice

Editor-in-Chief
Sharon Coan, M.S.Ed.

Creative Director
Lee Aucoin

Illustration Manager
Timothy J. Bradley

Publisher
Rachelle Cracchiolo, M.S.Ed.

Science Consultant
Scot Oschman, Ph.D.

Teacher Created Materials

5301 Oceanus Drive
Huntington Beach, CA 92649-1030
http://www.tcmpub.com
ISBN 978-1-4333-0314-2
© 2010 Teacher Created Materials, Inc.

Table of Contents

The First Fire

Ancient Greeks told a story to explain how people first got fire.

Prometheus (pruh-MEE-thee-uhs) was a powerful being. He made people from water and earth. Then he gave them many gifts. He gave them wisdom, strength, and all they would need for a happy life. But he wanted to give them more.

Zeus (zoohs) was the leader of the gods. Zeus ruled the sky and carried lightning bolts. Prometheus stole fire from one of Zeus's bolts. He gave it to the people. This made Zeus angry. Zeus punished Prometheus. He was chained to a mountain where an eagle ate his liver day after day. But now, people had a gift from the gods. They had fire.

Fennel

The story says that Prometheus hid the fire in a stalk of fennel. That is how he was able to bring fire to the people without the gods knowing.

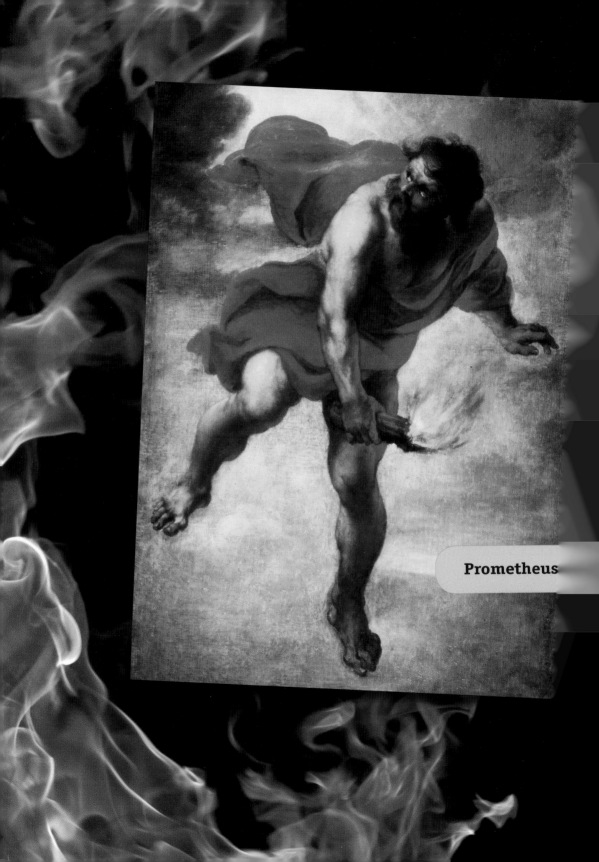

Prometheus

What Is Fire?

Fire is a state or process in which a fuel is **ignited** (set on fire) and gives off light, heat, and flame. That is why fire is very useful to people. They can use it for light and warmth. But fire can also be dangerous and even deadly.

Fire needs three things to exist. First, it must have **oxygen** (OK-si-juhn). Oxygen is the gas that makes up about one-fifth of our air.

Second, it needs **fuel**. Fuel is the substance that **combusts**. To combust is to catch fire. Fuel can be many things. Wood is a common fuel for fire. Gasoline is another one. Paper, cloth, and many gases can also be fuels.

The third thing a fire needs is **heat**. There must be enough heat to raise the temperature of the fuel. At a certain temperature, the fuel will ignite.

Fuel to the Fire

"Adding fuel to the fire" is an old expression. When people say it, they mean that someone is making a situation worse. By saying or doing something that gets someone else angry, they are making a problem more troublesome.

Phlogiston

Long ago, people thought that every combustible material had phlogiston (floh-JIS-ton) in it. They believed that fire was caused by the release of phlogiston. By the late 1700s, scientists knew this was not true.

OXYGEN HEAT FUEL

Fire needs these three elements to exist.

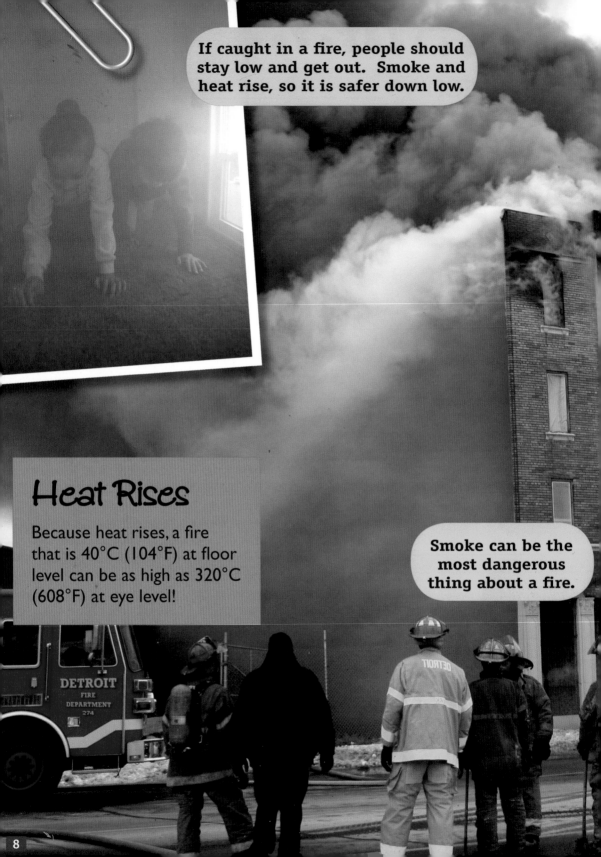

If caught in a fire, people should stay low and get out. Smoke and heat rise, so it is safer down low.

Heat Rises

Because heat rises, a fire that is 40°C (104°F) at floor level can be as high as 320°C (608°F) at eye level!

Smoke can be the most dangerous thing about a fire.

The U.S. Fire Administration describes fire in four ways: fast, hot, dark, and deadly.

Fire is so fast that a small fire can be out of control in less than a minute. It takes just a few minutes for a whole house to fill with smoke or go up in flames. If caught in a fire, a person should get out fast.

Fire is so hot that clothes can melt to a person's skin. Breathing the hot air can burn a person's lungs. The heat can even make a room ignite.

Fire gives light, but it can quickly make a room dark. That is because it creates thick, black smoke. It may be impossible to see in a fire.

And, of course, fire can be deadly. Even if the flames of a fire do not burn a person, the smoke and gases from a fire can kill him or her. Fire also uses up the oxygen in a room. People need oxygen to breathe. Lack of oxygen can make a person sleepy. He or she may not be able to wake up when a fire is near.

Flashover

When a whole area ignites all at once because of high heat, it is called a **flashover**.

Chemical Reaction

Ancient Greeks thought there were four main elements. They were earth, water, air, and fire. But they were wrong. Fire is not really like the other three. Earth, water, and air are all forms of **matter**. Matter is what every object is made of. But fire is not matter. Fire is a sign of matter changing form. It is part of a **chemical reaction.**

Substances that make up matter may react to one another. Something happens. The substances change. That is a chemical reaction. A new substance may be made. For example, iron and oxygen react to form rust. Fuel, oxygen, and a heat source form fire.

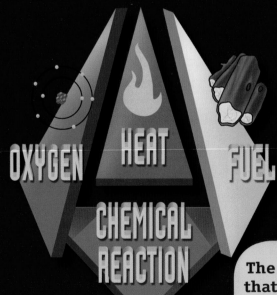

OXYGEN HEAT FUEL

CHEMICAL REACTION

The chemical reaction that creates fire needs fuel, oxygen, and a heat source to occur.

air

fire

water

earth

Physical Change or Chemical Reaction?

A substance can change its state, but that does not make it a chemical reaction. For example, water can freeze and become ice. That is just a physical change. It can be heated and become vapor. That is a physical change, too. But if water is separated into the two gases that make it (hydrogen and oxygen), that is a sign of a chemical reaction.

Fire is not like air, water, and earth. It is really a sign of a chemical reaction.

Colors

Fire can burn in different colors. The coolest fires burn red. The hottest fires burn violet. We cannot easily see the colors of the hottest fires, though. They usually just appear white to us.

After a fire, we can see the effects of the fire. Objects are burned. But is it really the object itself that burns? Not really. It is the gases given off from the object that do.

Heat raises temperature. The heated object gives off **flammable** gases. Flammable means "easily set on fire." When hot enough, the object ignites. There is fire. The fire creates more heat. It can keep itself going, as long as there is fuel (gas) and oxygen.

A chemical reaction happens. The object changes. When the fuel (gas) is used up, the object has been turned to ash or other particles.

You can see the effects of the chemical reactions after a fire has burned.

Take a Look

If you look closely at the flame of a candle, you will see that the wick is not really burning. There is no flame in the area just touching the wick. The gases close to the wick are too dense. They don't let in enough oxygen to burn. A little farther out, there are gases (fuel) and oxygen, as well as heat. This is where the fire is.

flame

dense gas

Importance of Fire in Nature

People can be fearful of fire. They want to stay safe. But fire is an important part of nature.

Many **ecosystems** depend on fire. Fire removes dead growth. It clears shade from the canopy level of forests. This allows plants on the forest floor to grow. Fire thins overgrowth and diseased plants so that other plants can spread out. New types of plants are able to take root. Regrowth has begun.

People from long ago let fire take its course. They knew that natural fire was good for the plants and the land. They also learned to use fire to help them with their needs. They used fire to clear land and keep roads open. They used it to increase fruit growth by bringing nutrients to the land. They used it to keep game in one area for hunting.

Fire Is Not for Everyone

Some ecosystems do not depend on fires. For example, deserts do not. A desert fire should be put out quickly.

Wildfires

A **wildfire** is an unplanned and unwanted fire in nature that causes a great deal of damage. Sometimes, these fires are started by nature. But nine times out of ten, they are caused by human carelessness.

Many ecosystems could not survive without natural fires.

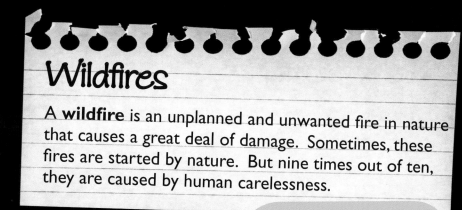

Fire allows for new growth to prosper.

People also set some fires so that natural fires would not be too harmful. Nature would have less to clean up. People worked with nature in this way.

But later, people did not want fire to get in their way. They did not know its importance to nature. They just saw that it ruined their homes and crops. So, they worked to stop each fire that nature started.

Yet populations grew, and so did the numbers of fires. People could not fight nature. Huge fires in the late 1800s were more than they could manage. More than one million acres were wiped out. Thousands of people were killed.

In 1988, more than 230 wildfires struck Yellowstone National Park and the area around it. People once tried to stop many fires from burning there. But these fires were more than they could control. They saw that they must work with nature. They must allow some burning to take place.

American Indians from long ago knew the importance of fire.

Why So Many Fires Today?

In the past several years, there has been a large amount of land burned. There are a few reasons for this. First, people once tried to stop all natural fires. This let a lot of overgrowth and dead plant material pile up. Second, the weather has been dry and hot. Third, weather patterns have been changing. And fourth, more people live close to wildlands, and people can be the greatest threat to nature.

The Yellowstone fires burned more than a million acres. Hundreds of animals and two people were killed. The fires burned for many weeks until snow began to fall.

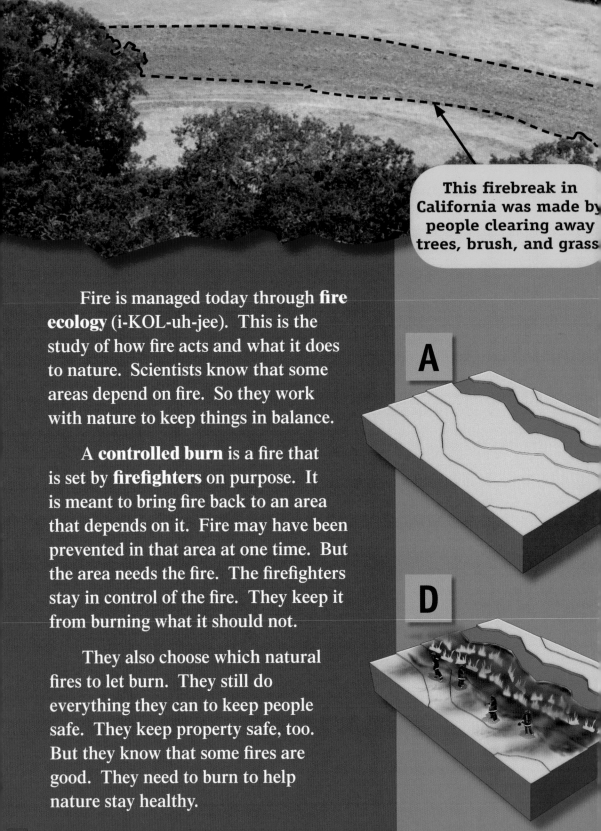

This firebreak in California was made by people clearing away trees, brush, and grass

Fire is managed today through **fire ecology** (i-KOL-uh-jee). This is the study of how fire acts and what it does to nature. Scientists know that some areas depend on fire. So they work with nature to keep things in balance.

A **controlled burn** is a fire that is set by **firefighters** on purpose. It is meant to bring fire back to an area that depends on it. Fire may have been prevented in that area at one time. But the area needs the fire. The firefighters stay in control of the fire. They keep it from burning what it should not.

They also choose which natural fires to let burn. They still do everything they can to keep people safe. They keep property safe, too. But they know that some fires are good. They need to burn to help nature stay healthy.

A

D

Creating a Controlled Burn

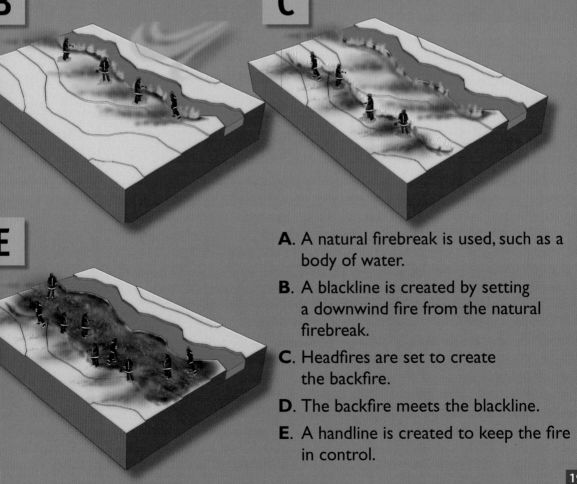

A. A natural firebreak is used, such as a body of water.

B. A blackline is created by setting a downwind fire from the natural firebreak.

C. Headfires are set to create the backfire.

D. The backfire meets the blackline.

E. A handline is created to keep the fire in control.

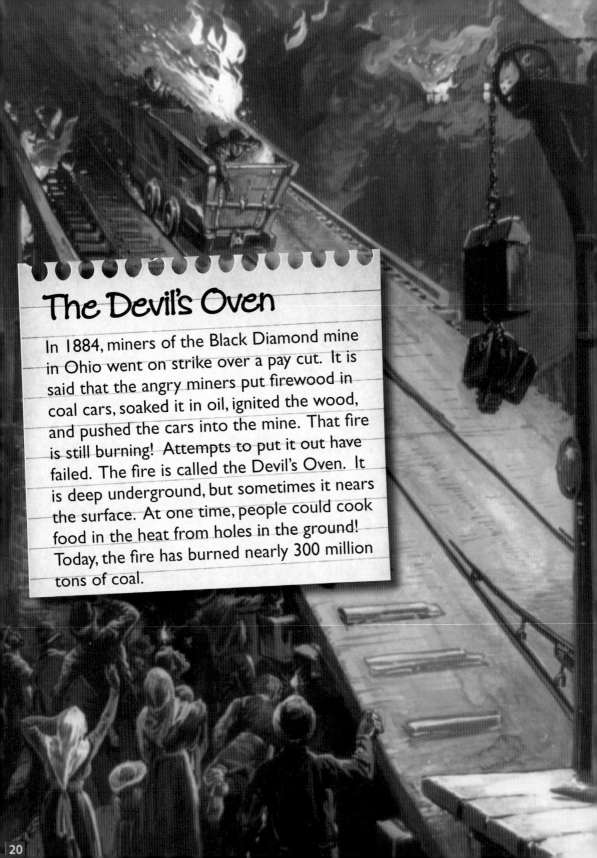

The Devil's Oven

In 1884, miners of the Black Diamond mine in Ohio went on strike over a pay cut. It is said that the angry miners put firewood in coal cars, soaked it in oil, ignited the wood, and pushed the cars into the mine. That fire is still burning! Attempts to put it out have failed. The fire is called the Devil's Oven. It is deep underground, but sometimes it nears the surface. At one time, people could cook food in the heat from holes in the ground! Today, the fire has burned nearly 300 million tons of coal.

Effects of Fire on Land

It is easy to see the effects of fire on the land's surface. Trees and shrubs are burned. Sometimes, buildings are destroyed, too. But the land itself is also affected. This can cause problems later on.

Fire burns at three levels in nature. A crown fire burns the tops of trees and plants. A surface fire burns plants at ground level. It clears away dead brush. A ground fire burns through soil that is rich with plant life. A wildfire may burn at one, two, or all three levels. Each of these levels has a different effect on what happens next.

crown fire

surface fire

ground fire

Crown fires burn plant life that is overhead. This lets sunlight through for plants that need it. It even helps the tallest plants by allowing sunlight to reach their seedlings.

Surface fires burn away dead and living growth. Some of these plants die off. But some protect their seeds and are able to grow anew. Some plants that have been burned are able to regrow. Some plants even need fire to survive. For example, the seeds of some plants with oil-coated leaves sprout through the heat of the fire. The new plants may take over areas where other plants have burned away.

There are some tall trees that resist the fire. That is because the parts that may burn are high above the fire level. The ponderosa pine is like this. It loses its lower branches as it grows. It often survives a mild natural fire.

The seeds of some plants begin to bud because of smoke and fire. For example, the cones of the lodgepole pine are coated with a resin. Fire melts the resin. This lets out the seeds.

Animal Survival

Animals must escape a fire to live. Most mammals and birds are able to flee. Birds are usually the first ones back after a fire. Amphibians may stay safe in water or wet mud. Reptiles often burrow during fires. Insects and spiders can find shelter, but they are sometimes drawn to the heat and die. Microbes may survive deep in the soil. After a fire, there may be more microbes than before. That is because a fire can produce the rich nutrients they like.

After the fire, sunlight is able to reach this conifer seedling.

The loss of plants during a ground fire has an effect on the land itself. The sun heats soil more easily. There is less shade to protect it. This changes what plants can grow there.

Also, more water seeps into the ground when rains come. That is because there are fewer plants to absorb the water. Plants also help water soak into the ground slowly. There are also fewer plants to keep the soil in place. So, **erosion** happens much easier after a fire.

One of the greatest dangers after fires are the **landslides** that often follow them. Imagine a hillside where a fire has been. The hill has lost all its plant life. There is nothing to keep the soil in place. And there is nothing to keep all the rain from soaking into the ground. A section of that hillside may easily slip away after a big rain. Even small parts of the hill will be changed as rain and winds come. Plants help prevent erosion. Fire makes erosion more likely.

No, Thank You!

Sometimes after a fire, soil won't let any water soak into it. That is because the high heat of the fire affects the soil. It makes the soil **repel** water instead of receive it.

Landslides and mudslides can be common side effects of heavy rainfall after a wildfire. The dotted red lines here show the path of a landslide after a Colorado wildfire.

Fire Safety

If you are caught in a fire, get out first. Then get help. You and your family should always have a plan for getting out of your home in case of a fire. Know where you will meet once you get out. And be sure to have working smoke alarms in your home. As Smokey says, "Always be careful!"

Change the batteries in your smoke alarms at least one time each year.

Always Be Careful!

Smokey Bear is a character that was created in 1944. He was made to tell people about the dangers of wildfire. He tells them how to stay safe and keep fires from starting.

Today we know that some fire is needed. We should not stop all fires. But we also should not start them. Do not play with matches. Do not walk away from campfires. Be smart and be safe. Follow Smokey's ABCs: Always **B**e **C**areful. Let nature—and the firefighters—take care of the rest.

Smokey Bear is the longest running public service campaign in the United States.

Lab: Eroding Earth

Erosion can result after fires or floods have swept through an area. This lab activity will help you to see what happens.

Materials

➡ dry, loose soil
➡ cheesecloth
➡ spray bottle and water, or hose with sprayer and a water source
➡ digital camera (optional)

Procedure:

1. Using dry loose soil, build a small steep hill about .6 meters (2 feet) across.

2. If a digital camera is available, take a photo of the hill to help with your observation.

3. Completely cover the hill with cheesecloth.

4. Take another photo of the hill, if a camera is available.

5. Using a sprinkler or a misting sprayer attached to a hose, apply water to the cloth-covered hill for a short time and watch what happens. Take photos during the spraying and after. Does the hill lose its shape? What happens to the soil? Does everything just stay in place but only get wet?

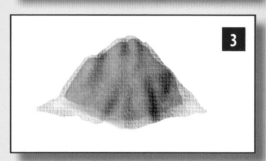

6. Remove the cheesecloth. (This is similar to what happens when vegetation is removed from a hill or mountainside.) Take another photo.

7. Using the sprinkler or misting sprayer attached to a hose, apply water to the hill again for a short time and watch what happens. Take photos during and after. What happens to the soil? What happens to the hill? Does everything stay in place?

8. What can you conclude, based on your experiment?

Glossary

chemical reaction—when the substances that make matter (molecules) react to one another and something happens

combust—ignite and burn

controlled burn—a fire set on purpose by firefighters to clear brush and to help the land, but is also prevented from getting out of hand

ecosystem—an area in nature that is formed by the relationships among all the plants and animals living there and by the land itself

erosion—the wearing away of land and rock by wind and water

fire ecology—the study of what fire does and its effects on the environment

firefighter—a worker whose job it is to control and put out fires in nature and in buildings

flammable—easily set on fire

flashover—combustion of a whole area all at once due to high heat

fuel—a substance that can be ignited and burned

heat—the state of having warmth

ignite—set on fire

landslide—the downward fall of soil, rocks, and debris from a hillside

matter—the substance that makes up every physical object; commonly defined as anything having mass and taking up space

oxygen—a natural gas that makes up a large portion of Earth's atmosphere

repel—resist; force away

substance—the stuff that makes up something

wildfire—a damaging and unplanned fire in nature

Index

Scientists Then and Now

Wladimir Köppen
(1846–1940)

Jagdish Shukla
(1944–)

Wladimir Köppen grew up in Russia. He studied botany, climate, and weather. As an adult, he traveled a lot. He saw that the places he visited had very different types of plants. These differences made him curious. So, he studied the differences and found that temperature had big effects on plants. He developed the Köppen climate classification system. This system is still used by scientists.

Jagdish Shukla was born in a small village in India. He wanted to study science in school, but his school did not teach it. His father got science books for him, and Shukla taught himself. Today, he is a science professor and does research on weather and climate. He has helped people to better understand the weather and climates of the world. He has received many important awards for his work.

Image Credits